MR. STRONG

by Roger Hargreaves

This is the story of Mr Strong.

Mr Strong is the strongest person in the whole wide world.

The strongest person there ever has been, and probably the strongest person there ever will be.

He is so strong he can not only bend an iron bar with his bare hands, he can tie knots in it!

Mr Strong is so strong he can throw a cannonball as far as you or I can throw a tennis ball!

Mr Strong is so strong he can hammer nails into a wall just by tapping them with his finger.

Strong by name and strong by nature!

And would you like to know the secret of Mr Strong's strength?

Eggs!

The more eggs Mr Strong eats, the stronger he becomes.

Stronger and stronger and stronger!

Anyway, this story is about a funny thing that happened to Mr Strong one day.

That morning he was having breakfast.

And for breakfast he was having . . .eggs!

Followed by eggs. And to finish, he was having – guess what?

That's right. Eggs!

That was Mr Strong's normal breakfast.

After his eggy breakfast Mr Strong cleaned his teeth.

And, as usual, he squeezed all the toothpaste out of the tube.

And, as usual, he cleaned his teeth so hard he broke his toothbrush.

Mr Strong gets through a lot of toothpaste and toothbrushes!

After that he decided to take a walk.

He put on his hat and opened the front door of his house. Crash!

"What a beautiful day," he thought to himself and, stepping outside his house, he shut his front door.

Bang! The door fell off its hinges.

Mr Strong gets through a lot of front doors!

Then Mr Strong went for his walk.

He walked through the woods.

But, he wasn't looking where he was going, and walked slap bang into a huge tree. Crack!

The huge tree trunk snapped and the tree thundered to the ground.

"Whoops!" said Mr Strong.

He walked into town.

And again, not looking where he was going, he walked slap bang straight into a bus.

Now, as you know, if you or I were to walk into a bus, we'd get run over.

Wouldn't we?

Not Mr Strong!

The bus stopped as if it had run into a brick wall.

"Whoops!" said Mr Strong.

Eventually Mr Strong walked through the town and out into the country. To a farm.

The farmer met him in the road looking very worried.

"What's the matter?" asked Mr Strong.

"It's my cornfield," replied the farmer. "It's on fire and I can't put it out!"

Mr Strong looked over the hedge, and sure enough the cornfield was blazing fiercely.

"Water," said Mr Strong. "We must get water to put out the fire!"

"But I don't have enough water to put a whole field out," cried the worried farmer, "and the nearest water is down at the river, and I don't have a pump!"

"Then we'll have to find something to carry the water," replied Mr Strong.

"Is that your barn?" he asked the farmer, pointing to a barn in another field.

"Yes, I was going to put my corn in it," said the farmer. "But . . ."

"Can I use it?" asked Mr Strong.

"Yes, but . . .," replied the perplexed farmer.

Mr Strong walked over to the barn, and then do you know what he did?

He picked it up. He actually picked up the barn!

The farmer couldn't believe his eyes.

Then Mr Strong carried the barn, above his head, down to the river.

Then he turned the barn upside down.

Then he lowered it into the river so that it filled up with water.

Then, and this shows how strong Mr Strong is, he picked it up and carried it back to the blazing cornfield.

Mr Strong emptied the upside down barn full of water over the flames.

Sizzle. Sizzle. Splutter. Splutter.

One minute the flames were leaping into the air. The next minute they'd gone.

"However can I thank you?" the farmer asked Mr Strong.

"Oh, it was nothing," remarked Mr Strong modestly.

"But I must find some way to reward you," said the farmer.

"Well," said Mr Strong, "you're a farmer, so you must keep chickens."

"Yes, lots," said the farmer.

"And chickens lay eggs," went on Mr Strong, "and I rather like eggs!"

"Then you shall have as many eggs as you can carry," said the farmer, and took Mr Strong over to the farmyard.

Mr Strong said goodbye to the farmer, and thanked him for the eggs, and the farmer thanked him for helping.

Then Mr Strong, just using one finger, picked up the eggs and went home.

Mr Strong put the eggs carefully down on his kitchen table and went to close the kitchen door.

Crash! The door fell off its hinges.

"Whoops!" said Mr Strong, and sat down.

Crunch! The chair fell to bits.

"Whoops!" said Mr Strong, and started cooking his lunch. And for lunch he was starting with eggs. Followed by an egg or two. And then eggs. And then for his pudding he was having . . .

Well, can you guess? If you can, there's no need to turn this page over to find out that he was having . . .

Ice cream!

Ha! Ha!

3 Great Offers For Mr Men Fans

1 Token
EGMONT WORLD

1 FREE Door Hangers and Posters

In every Mr Men and Little Miss Book like this one you will find a special token. Collect 6 and we will send you either a brilliant Mr. Men or Little Miss poster and a Mr Men or Little Miss double sided, full colour, bedroom door hanger. Apply using the coupon overleaf, enclosing six tokens and a 50p coin for your choice of two items.

Egmont World tokens can be used towards any other Egmont World / World International token scheme promotions, in early learning and story / activity books.

Posters: Tick your preferred choice of either Mr Men ☐ or Little Miss ☐

Door Hangers: Choose from: Mr. Nosey & Mr Muddle ☐, Mr Greedy & Mr Lazy ☐, Mr Tickle & Mr Grumpy ☐, Mr Slow & Mr Busy ☐ Mr Messy & Mr Quiet ☐, Mr Perfect & Mr Forgetful ☐, Little Miss Fun & Little Miss Late ☐, Little MIss Helpful & Little Miss Tidy ☐, Little Miss Busy & Little Miss Brainy ☐, Little Miss Star & Little Miss Fun ☐.
(Please tick)

2 Mr Men Library Boxes

Keep your growing collection of Mr Men and Little Miss books in these superb library boxes. With an integral carrying handle and stay-closed fastener, these full colour, plastic boxes are fantastic. They are just £5.49 each including postage. Order overleaf.

3 Join The Club

To join the fantastic Mr Men & Little Miss Club, check out the page overleaf NOW!

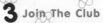

MR MEN and LITTLE MISS™ & © 1998 Mrs. Roger Hargreaves

Join Our Club!

MR. MEN & little miss CLUB

When you become a member of the fantastic Mr Men and Little Miss Club you'll receive a personal letter from Mr Happy and Little Miss Giggles, a club badge with your name, and a superb Welcome Pack (pictured below right).

You'll also get birthday and Christmas cards from the Mr Men and Little Misses, 2 newsletters crammed with special offers, privileges and news, and a copy of the 12 page Mr Men catalogue which includes great party ideas.

If it were on sale in the shops, the Welcome Pack alone might cost around £13. But a year's membership is just £9.99 (plus 73p postage) with a 14 day money-back guarantee if you are not delighted!

HOW TO APPLY To apply for any of these three great offers, ask an adult to complete the coupon below and send it with appropriate payment and tokens (where required) to: Mr Men Offers, PO Box 7, Manchester M19 2HD. Credit card orders for Club membership ONLY by telephone, please call: 01403 242727.

To be completed by an adult

❏ **1.** Please send a poster and door hanger as selected overleaf. I enclose six tokens and a 50p coin for post (coin not required if you are also taking up 2. or 3. below).

❏ **2.** Please send __ Mr Men Library case(s) and __ Little Miss Library case(s) at £5.49 each.

❏ **3.** Please enrol the following in the Mr Men & Little Miss Club at £10.72 (inc postage)

Fan's Name:_____ Fan's Address:_____

_____ Post Code:_____ Date of birth:___/___/___

Your Name:_____ Your Address:_____

Post Code:_____ Name of parent or guardian (if not you):_____

Total amount due: £_____ (£5.49 per Library Case, £10.72 per Club membership)

❏ I enclose a cheque or postal order payable to Egmont World Limited.

❏ Please charge my MasterCard / Visa account.

Card number: | | | | | | | | | | | | | | | | |

Expiry Date: ____/____   Signature: _____

Data Protection Act: If you do **not** wish to receive other family offers from us or companies we recommend, please tick this box ❏. Offer applies to UK only